STAR WARS®

THE FORCE AWAKENS

Adapted by Christopher Nicholas
Illustrated by Caleb Meurer and Micky Rose

 A GOLDEN BOOK • NEW YORK

randomhousekids.com
ISBN 978-0-7364-3491-1 (trade) — ISBN 978-0-7364-3492-8 (ebook)
Printed in the United States of America
10 9 8 7 6 5 4

A long time ago in a galaxy far, far away . . .

Thirty years after the fall of the evil Empire, an army known as the **First Order** threatens to take over the galaxy. General Leia Organa, leader of the Resistance, needs help to restore peace. So Leia sends daring X-wing pilot **Poe Dameron** and his faithful droid **BB-8** on a special mission to find a map that leads to her brother—Luke Skywalker, the last of the Jedi.

Poe and BB-8 travel to the planet Jakku, where they retrieve the map from Leia's old friend Lor San Tekka. Suddenly, the First Order attacks! Commander **Kylo Ren** and an army of **stormtroopers** capture Lor and Poe. Luckily, the pilot hid the map in BB-8 and sent the droid to find help.

BB-8 **escapes** into the desert.
But the droid is soon trapped by an
angry Teedo riding a luggabeast.

A young scavenger named **Rey** feels bad
for the droid and rescues BB-8. Rey doesn't
have a family, and BB-8 is clearly lost, so
she agrees to let the droid stay with her.

Meanwhile, on board a First Order **Star Destroyer**, Kylo Ren uses the **Force**—a powerful energy field—to make Poe reveal that BB-8 has the map. The brave Resistance pilot is about to give up hope when he is rescued by a stormtrooper!

FN-2187 doesn't want to fight for the First Order anymore and offers to **help** Poe escape.

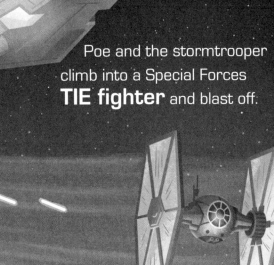

Poe and the stormtrooper climb into a Special Forces **TIE fighter** and blast off.

"I'm calling you **Finn**. That all right?" Poe says to FN-2187.

Just then, the Star Destroyer fires on the TIE, sending Poe and Finn **crashing** down to Jakku.

Finn can't find any sign of Poe among the TIE fighter wreckage. So he sets off and soon finds the pilot's droid and Rey at an outpost. Finn tells Rey about Poe and BB-8's **special mission** for the Resistance. Suddenly, stormtroopers appear and try to capture the trio!

Finn, Rey, and BB-8
race aboard an old space
freighter and **blast off**.
First Order TIE fighters
chase after them.

As Finn climbs into the gunner's seat, Rey pilots
the freighter through an old Star Destroyer wreck.
Zoom! The heroes escape into space.

Unfortunately, the freighter is damaged
during the wild chase. Rey makes repairs while
Finn asks BB-8 to reveal the location of the
secret Resistance base. Suddenly, the freighter
is caught in a **tractor beam**—and sucked
into the cargo bay of a **massive ship**!

Rey, Finn, and BB-8 hide under a grating.
But they are quickly discovered by a tall man and a
Wookiee. It is **Han Solo** and his copilot, **Chewbacca**—
heroes of the Rebel Alliance that helped defeat the evil
Empire years ago!

"Chewie, we're home," Han says to his furry friend. They are thrilled to finally have their stolen ship, the *Millennium Falcon,* back again.

Rey and Finn are eager to deliver BB-8 and the map to the Resistance base. But first Han and Chewbacca have to deal with some **uninvited** guests—the **Kanjiklub** and the **Guavian Death Gang!**

Han owes both gangs money,
and they are eager to **collect**.

Rey wants to help, so she tries to close the blast doors and trap the gangs. But instead she accidentally releases Han and Chewie's cargo—**vicious creatures** called **rathtars**! It is just the distraction Han and Chewbacca need to make their escape. Together with Rey, Finn, and BB-8, they blast off in the *Falcon*.

Meanwhile, Kylo Ren returns to the stronghold of the First Order. Located on an ice planet, **Starkiller Base** is armed with a superweapon strong enough to destroy an entire solar system!

Kylo Ren immediately reports to his master, **Supreme Leader Snoke**.

"The droid we seek is aboard the *Millennium Falcon*, once again piloted by Han Solo," Snoke snarls.

"No one will stand in our way," Kylo Ren vows.

Before flying to the Resistance base, Han Solo lands on the planet Takodana to get help from a friend. **Maz** is a wise old alien who lives in a grand castle.

Maz tries to give Rey a special gift—Luke Skywalker's old **lightsaber**, a powerful laser sword. But when the young scavenger touches it, she has a **vision** of pain and suffering and runs off. So Maz asks Finn to take the lightsaber and keep it for Rey.

A **spy** in Maz's castle alerts Kylo Ren, and soon First Order stormtroopers attack!

Rey puts up a brave fight but is **captured** by Kylo Ren and taken aboard his transport.

Han and Chewie fire their blasters at approaching stormtroopers. Finn ignites the lightsaber and joins the battle.

Suddenly, a squadron of Resistance X-wing fighters—led by Poe Dameron—**zooms** in and **saves the day**! Kylo Ren and his troops retreat to Starkiller Base with Rey.

Back at the Resistance base, General Leia Organa and her team come up with a **plan** to destroy the Starkiller and rescue Rey.

Han, Chewbacca, and Finn fly the *Falcon* to the First Order base and **sneak** inside. The trio quickly disable the Starkiller's shields.

But as they try to find Rey's prison cell, they discover she has already escaped on her own. Reunited, the heroes begin placing **explosive** charges in the Starkiller's cooling system.

Suddenly, a **dark figure** appears! Kylo Ren removes his helmet—and reveals that he is really Han and Leia's son, Ben Solo! Han begs Ben to leave the First Order and come home with him. But Kylo Ren has been turned to evil by Supreme Leader Snoke. The villain ignites his red lightsaber and sends his father tumbling down into a **deep pit**!

Chewbacca fires his bowcaster, injuring Kylo Ren and giving the **heroes** a chance to escape.

As Rey and Finn race across the frozen planet toward the *Falcon*, Kylo Ren **catches up** with them! The villain knocks Rey unconscious, but Finn wields Luke Skywalker's lightsaber to protect his friend. Unfortunately, the former stormtrooper is no match for Kylo Ren and is quickly **defeated**.

But before Kylo Ren can deliver the final blow, Rey awakens and uses the **Force** to levitate the blue lightsaber right into her hand!

With the Force as her ally, the young scavenger reveals herself to be a **powerful** warrior. The lightsaber battle comes to a sudden end when **explosions** create a deep crater between Rey and Kylo Ren.

Chewbacca flies in on the *Millennium Falcon* and helps Rey carry the injured Finn on board. The heroes blast off—just as Poe Dameron and his X-wing squadron fire their torpedoes at the Starkiller! The First Order's **superweapon** is destroyed!

KA-BOOM!

Beep- bop -bOop!

Back at the Resistance base, BB-8 projects the star map to Luke Skywalker's location. Unfortunately, a crucial part is missing. Luke Skywalker's old astromech droid, **R2-D2**, suddenly reactivates—and reveals the final piece of the map!

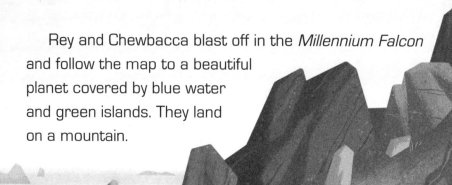

Rey and Chewbacca blast off in the *Millennium Falcon* and follow the map to a beautiful planet covered by blue water and green islands. They land on a mountain.

Rey climbs a stone staircase and meets a hooded figure. The figure lowers his hood, revealing the face of . . .

Luke Skywalker! Rey hands the Jedi Master his old lightsaber.

There has been an **awakening** in the Force—and young Rey knows that she has an exciting future ahead of her!